The Girl with Green Hair

by Janet Adele Bloss

illustrated by Clovis Martin

To my brother and sister Xenoids—
with love and gratitude
and
To Roger and Lynn Brucker
and the Beaver Creek Family—
with special thanks

"What we ardently love we learn to imitate."

Ralph Waldo Emerson, April 18, 1824

Published by Willowisp Press, Inc.
401 E. Wilson Bridge Road, Worthington, Ohio 43085

Copyright © 1989 by Willowisp Press, Inc.

Printed in the United States of America
10 9 8 7 6 5 4 3 2

ISBN 0-87406-416-3

One

MOST girls my age seem to have the usual problems. You know the kind of problems I mean—a pesty little sister, a bossy older brother, a bad grade on a report card, big feet, or weird parents.

But not me. I get *B*s in school. I don't have a little sister. My older brother, Michael, is really nice most of the time. And my parents hardly ever get angry with me. So, I guess that that means they love me.

Sometimes it's hard, though, when you have a brother who does everything as great as my brother does. I mean, he's nice and he's smart. He was the best swimmer on his high school team, too. My parents always seem to be so proud of Michael. And next year he is going away to college. He even won a swimming scholarship to pay for his classes. I wish I was paid to go to school!

You should hear Mom and Dad tell everyone about Michael. It seems like they talk about him a lot. They never seem to talk about me. But I have to admit that I haven't done anything very special for them to talk about—*yet*. After all, I'm only 12 years old and going into the seventh grade this fall.

I wish I could figure out what *I*, Cassie Young, am really good at. I want my parents to think that I am as special as Michael is. Their favorite thing about me seems to be my long, blond hair. At least, my hair used to be blond! It's naturally wavy and falls halfway down my back. A lot of people think it's pretty. But my hair's not really something I want to be known for. I want to *do* something that will make me stand out.

That brings me to the real problem. I do

stand out now. But it's not because of any trophy that I've won or something important that I've done. It's because I have green hair! Yes, I really have green hair!

It all started when I joined the Aqua Bears swim team a couple of weeks ago. I wanted to be a good swimmer like Michael. Right now he's away at swimming camp for a month. Mom and Dad call him a lot to hear about all the wonderful things he's doing. Then they tell me all about him. And—I admit it—I'm jealous of him.

So, that's why I decided to join the Swimland swim team. The pool is close enough to my house so that I can walk there. And I talked my best friend, Robin, into joining the team with me. It was easy to convince her. I just told her that it would be a great way to meet boys. You see, Robin is sort of boy crazy. I've seen this mushy boy stuff creeping up on her for a long time. She starts giggling whenever she's around a boy she likes. It's weird.

My plan was to work out at the pool every day. I figured that the more I worked out, the faster I would improve and win trophies. And then my parents would be proud of me, too.

But things didn't go the way I'd planned. I talked to my swim coach, Mrs. Jordan, about my hair at first. She said that the chlorine in the pool can turn hair green. It doesn't happen to everyone's hair.

Mrs. Jordan said Robin's hair won't change color because hers is red. But my hair is beginning to look like pea soup. Mom and Dad haven't noticed it yet, but it won't be long before they do. And then they'll be really angry with me for ruining my blond hair.

But I just can't quit the swim team, because I have to be as good as my brother. And besides that, my parents would think I'm a quitter.

I sneak out of the house early in the morning so that my parents don't see my green hair. I run the few blocks to the pool. It makes me feel really refreshed to feel the crisp morning air pumping through my lungs. I eat my lunch outside in the sunshine beside the pool, and then I swim all afternoon.

I swim the breaststroke most of the time because that's what I'm best at. But Mrs. Jordan has us practice all the strokes so we know them all.

Karl Bosley is captain of the boys' team, and Lanna Baker is captain of the girls' team. Lanna is the best girl swimmer. I'd love to beat her sometime, but so far Robin is the only one I can beat.

When I got home from the pool this after-noon, the first thing I did was run and look in the bathroom mirror. What a sight! My eyes were bloodshot, like a villain on a late night horror movie. And my hair was more green than ever!

I grabbed a scarf from the bottom of Mom's drawer and tied it over my hair. When Mom saw me, she looked at me strangely and asked

what I was up to.

I had to think fast. "It's really hot outside today, Mom. The scarf keeps my hair off my neck."

"But do you have to wear it in the house?" she asked.

She had me there. It took me a minute before I said, "I'm just being prepared for anything."

Mom didn't ask anything else, and I quickly took the plate of chicken salad and glass of milk that she handed me. As I sat at the kitchen table eating my snack, Mom opened the refrigerator to put the leftover salad back in. Then she stood there staring into the refrigerator.

"I'm still not used to being able to go into the refrigerator without worrying about spilling a glass of milk," Mom said finally. She was talking about Michael's habit of getting something to drink and then leaving an inch of liquid in the bottom of the glass. He always puts it back in the refrigerator—even though he never gets around to drinking it. Then someone else usually knocks over the glass and spills whatever was in it all over the refrigerator.

"But Mom, you always tell him to stop doing that!"

Mom smiled and closed the refrigerator door. "You're right. But it's funny how you can miss little things like that. Out of habit, I've even gone into the living room to pick up Michael's sneakers."

"You mean the smelly ones he leaves on the coffee table?" I asked disgustedly.

Mom nodded and grinned. "I know it's silly," she admitted. "But right now he's away at camp. And pretty soon he'll be going away to college." She reached out and patted the top of my head. Little did she know that under that scarf was my long, greenish hair.

"How's swimming?" Mom asked. "Do you like it?"

"Uh, yes," I lied. "It's great! But my times aren't good yet. I'm working hard to get better," I added eagerly.

"That's my girl," said Mom. Then she left to do some shopping. I knew what I had to do. *It's the only way*, I thought. I had to do everything Michael did so she wouldn't miss him. I could take his place if I tried hard enough. *Just wait and see*, I thought.

I poured a glass of orange pop, and I was careful to leave just an inch of liquid in the bottom of the glass. I put the glass on the top shelf like Michael usually does, and quickly closed the door.

I smiled to myself. If I can take his place, then Mom and Dad won't notice he's gone. Then I'd get all the attention. I went upstairs to my room to find my oldest pair of sneakers. They would be perfect on the coffee table in the living room. I ran down and plopped them right in the middle of the table. My plan would work in no time. I was sure of it.

Two

EVEN though it was really hot outside, I ran all the way to the pool. Robin was waiting for me near the lockers.

"That's a nice scarf," she said. "Is it a new style?"

"Oops! I forgot I had this on!" I exclaimed, pulling the scarf from my head. I saw Robin lean closer and stare at my hair.

She shook her head sadly. "Uh, it's still green, Cassie," she said.

"I know," I moaned. I grabbed my swim cap and pulled it over my head. I didn't want to talk about my hair anymore. We left the locker room and headed outside toward the pool. As soon as Robin saw Karl Bosley, she started giggling. How mushy!

I jumped as a wave of pool water came crashing into my face. "Oh, I'm sorry," said Joe Finnegan, another guy on our team. His fishy-looking eyes stared at me through goggles. I could tell he really wasn't sorry at all because he kept laughing.

I've decided the best thing to do with Joe is to ignore him. So, I looked away and pulled my goggles down over my eyes. Coach Jordan blew her whistle and instructed all of us to begin swimming laps.

With each stroke, it was like I could actually picture the water rushing underneath my bathing cap. I could feel the rush of the water and the chlorine. I almost could imagine my hair turning more green.

That night at dinner, Dad stared at me from across the table. "Cassie, what's that on your head?" he asked.

For a second, I thought maybe some hair was sticking out the bottom of my scarf. I reached up and felt for evidence. But the scarf was in place.

"Oh, this? It's a new style, Dad," I said. "All the girls are wearing scarves these days."

Mom looked surprised. "I thought you said the scarf was to keep the hair off your neck," she said.

"Well, yeah, that's why *I'm* wearing it," I explained. "But the other girls do it because it's the latest style."

Mom and Dad stared at me like I was an alien from Mars. Obviously, they hadn't noticed this new style anywhere. *I guess not too many people had*, I thought sarcastically.

Then Dad smiled. "You kids," he said. "What will you think of next?"

After that crisis had passed, I relaxed. Suddenly, Mom stood up and walked over to the counter. "Oh, I just remembered that we got a letter from Michael today. Do you want to hear it?" she asked.

Dad nodded. Mom pulled the letter from

its envelope and began to read. I scooped some more fried chicken from the plate in the center of the table. As I chewed, I listened to what Michael had to say.

Michael said that he swims twice a day and that some hotshot coach is at the camp. And, of course, he bragged about being just a half of a second away from the camp's best time for the freestyle category.

I stuffed part of a biscuit into my mouth. I noticed that Dad was listening intently to Mom. I could see the pride in Dad's face and hear it in Mom's voice as she read the letter.

Well, good old Michael has made Mom and Dad proud again, I thought. I wished that Michael could do something average for a change. I guess that every family has an average kid. But I'm tired of being the average kid in this family.

When Mom had finally finished reading, she carefully refolded the letter like it was made of gold. Then she and Dad started talking about Michael's success at camp.

Just in time, the phone rang. I jumped up and ran to the kitchen. It was Robin.

"Hi," she said after I had answered the phone. "Do you have a minute to talk?"

"Sure," I said. "What's up?"

"I'm quitting the Aqua Bears," Robin said bluntly.

"What?" I shrieked. "You can't leave! You're my best friend. You have to stay with me."

"It's not as much fun as I thought it'd be. And I look ugly wearing goggles. I'll never meet boys that way," Robin whined.

"So, don't wear them," I urged.

"But then my eyes get all red," complained Robin. "And the water is ruining my skin. I feel dry and itchy all the time."

"Rub on some lotion when you get out of the water," I suggested desperately.

"And I always smell like chlorine," Robin continued, ignoring my suggestions.

"Boys like girls who like sports," I reassured

her, forcing some enthusiasm into my voice.

"I don't know," Robin said hesitantly.

I only had one idea left. "What about Karl Bosley?" I asked. "I thought you liked him. And the Aqua Bears is the best way to see him, isn't it?"

"Uh, yeah," Robin agreed slowly.

"So, please stay on the team with me," I practically begged her.

There was silence for a few seconds.

"Oh, okay," Robin said at last. "I'll see how it goes for a little while longer."

I relaxed after she'd said that, and we talked about our usual things. Robin told me about her little sister who drives her crazy. And I told her about Michael's letter from camp. Maybe there should be a law that each family can only have one kid. But then I guess I wouldn't have been born.

After we had hung up, I went into my bedroom and looked into the mirror. My long pink scarf hung down over my hair. Lifting the tail of the scarf up, I peered under it.

There it was! My hair was still a gross green color. I'd been hoping that the green color would wear itself out of my hair and into the scarf or something. But no such luck.

I tied the scarf firmly under my chin. Suddenly, I heard the clanking of glass in the kitchen, and then I heard dad yell.

"Cassie, did you leave a glass of orange pop in here?" he asked angrily.

I pretended not to hear him.

"There's a sponge by the sink, Steve. You can mop it up with that," Mom told him.

I crept quietly back into my bedroom. *Dad never yells when Michael leaves his glass in the refrigerator*, I thought angrily. Mom and Dad think it's cute when he does it. It's just not fair!

I closed the door to my room. I tried to get my mind off of my problems by reading a chapter in an adventure book. I started to feel sleepy after a while, so I pulled on my pajamas and walked down the hall to the bathroom to brush my teeth.

"That's a pretty serious fashion statement you're making, Cassie," Dad said as he passed me in the hallway. He grinned, and I knew he was talking about the scarf on my head.

"Cassie," he said. "You know better than to leave a glass of pop in the refrigerator."

"Yeah, I know. I'm sorry, Dad," I mumbled as I disappeared into the bathroom and closed the door behind me.

If they only knew the truth, I thought. Mom and Dad would faint if they saw my green hair. They'd be the laughing stock of the neighborhood, of our whole town, and maybe of the whole state of California!

Oh, why does weird stuff like this always happen to me? I asked myself. I wanted to cry.

I stared at my reflection in the mirror and whispered, "You're average. You're just an average kid—an average kid with green hair!"

Usually, Mom and Dad have to make me go

to bed at night. I love staying up late to read or watch TV. But not tonight. I didn't want to face them or any more questions. So, I crawled into bed, carefully arranging the scarf so that it wouldn't come off during the night.

I heard the door to my bedroom open. I pretended to be asleep. Mom's voice whispered in the dark. "Shhh, she's asleep."

"Does she still have that scarf on her head?" I heard Dad ask.

"Uh-huh," Mom answered.

"That's crazy. Do you think we can get the scarf off without waking her up?" asked Dad.

My heart froze as I heard footsteps approach the bed. What would they say when they discovered the awful truth? Would they scream? Would Mom faint?

A moment later, I felt Mom's lips kiss me on the forehead. Then quietly she and Dad left the room.

I was saved. But not for long.

Three

THE next day was bright and sunny. Dad was gone by the time I came out of my bedroom. I went into the kitchen, grabbed some cereal, and sat down at the table beside Mom. I was glad she didn't say anything about my scarf.

After breakfast I went upstairs to Michael's room. I like to do that sometimes when he's not home. There's a big photograph of him on the wall holding a large silver cup that his swim team won at the state championship last year.

Then there's the bulletin board covered with Michael's ribbons. Knowing my brother, he'd never take the time to pin all those ribbons up there in straight rows. Mom did it for him. Next are his trophies that are arranged on bookshelves beside his bed.

Looking around the room, I felt like I was in the swimming hall of fame. It seemed like every square inch of the room was filled with some sort of award.

Quietly, I returned to my own room and looked around. There were only books. And the pins on my bulletin board held up my favorite comic strips, a ticket to play a free game of miniature golf, and an autographed photo of a cute TV star.

I checked to be sure that my bedroom door was closed tightly before I pulled my scarf off. I walked over to the mirror and checked out my hair from all angles to see if the green had softened. It was still green. Well, it wasn't green-green. It was just greenish.

I wondered if I would have to spend the rest of my life hiding my hair. Then, suddenly, I knew what to do.

I'd work extra hard so that I would win a ribbon at my first competition. Then everything would be okay because Mom and Dad would be so proud of my ribbon that they wouldn't care about my weird-looking hair.

I looked at my watch and saw that Swimland would be opening soon. I quickly tied the scarf back over my hair. Then I grabbed my gym bag and ran downstairs.

"Bye, Mom!" I shouted. "I might be home for lunch."

I ran all the way to the pool. I passed the neighborhood kids who were playing with their toys on the sidewalk. I was breathing heavily by the time I reached the pool. Joe Finnegan was walking up the sidewalk.

"What's the rush?" Joe asked. "Are your feet on fire? Where did you get that dumb-looking scarf?"

"Buzz off!" I said. Then, tucking my gym bag under my arm, I hurried to the girl's locker room. Robin was waiting for me.

"There you are!" Robin exclaimed. "Oh, Cassie, I look terrible with these goggles on!" Her eyes stared out at me from behind thick plastic goggles.

"I think they look nice," I said. I wasn't going to let her talk about quitting the Aqua Bears again.

"But Karl Bosley will laugh at me!" she wailed. "How could any boy look at a girl with goggles?"

I whipped my pink scarf off and began stuffing my hair into my bathing cap. "You think you've got problems," I said. "How would you like to have green hair?"

Robin's face suddenly lighted up with a big smile. "Oh, I almost forgot!" she exclaimed. "I've got great news for you."

"They've picked swimmers for the competition?" I asked with a grin.

Robin shook her head vigorously. "No, it's better than that!" she squealed.

I waited anxiously for her to calm down so

I could hear what she had to say.

"It's about your hair!" Robin exclaimed. "I know how you can change the color. You won't have green hair anymore."

"Wh-what?" My mouth hung open.

Robin was all smiles. "I saw it in the drug store yesterday," she explained. "You can get a box of hair tint. It's easy. You just mix two bottles together and work it into your hair. It takes just a few minutes for your hair to change color."

I was skeptical. It all sounded too good to be true.

"You look at the hair color on the box to pick the one that you want," Robin insisted. "I saw a color that's exactly like the color your hair used to be."

This was beginning to sound better and better. I could be back to my own normal—I mean, average—self in no time!

"When can we do it?" I asked.

"We can do it tonight," Robin said. "Ask

your mom if you can spend the night with me. We'll buy a box of hair color, and then we'll dye your hair at my house."

Good old Robin had saved me again, I thought. Robin was my best friend in the whole world. We met in second grade, and we've been best friends ever since. We left the locker room and walked out into the bright sunshine. A bunch of kids our age were playing and splashing in the pool.

"How much does it cost?" I asked eagerly. I couldn't wait to get on with the dying.

"It costs about five dollars," said Robin. "It's expensive."

"But it's worth it," I added quickly. I didn't have very much money saved up in my bank at home, but I'd pay even more than five dollars just to have my normal hair back again.

As I swam laps back and forth across the pool, I tried to think about things that would make me happy, like winning a swimming trophy, making Mom and Dad proud of me, and having my own hair back again.

At noon, I decided to go home to eat lunch. I climbed out of the pool and headed to the locker room to change clothes. I was so happy about the hair-dying party that was coming up that night that I ran all the way home.

"Are you still wearing that scarf?" Mom asked as I walked in through the back door.

"Yeah," I admitted. "But I don't think I'll be wearing it after today."

"Why's that?" asked Mom.

"I don't think I like this style anymore," I said.

Mom just shook her head like she was thinking I was extremely weird. Then she opened the refrigerator door. I saw a small orange puddle on the top shelf and squirmed as I remembered Dad yelling in the kitchen last night when he knocked over my partially filled glass of pop.

"Mom, can I spend the night with Robin tonight?" I asked hopefully. *If she says no, I'll just die*, I thought.

"Sure, you can," said Mom. "Dad can drive you over there after dinner."

I settled back into my chair and took a big bite out of the ham sandwich that Mom had given me.

"Cassie," said Mom. She leaned across the table looking deeply into my eyes. "Is there something on your mind? Is there anything you want to talk about?"

"Uh...why do you ask?" I asked, suddenly choking on a piece of ham.

Because I keep finding your sneakers in the strangest places. Yesterday, they were on the coffee table. Today, they were on the TV. I've been trying for ages to get Michael to be neater, like you. But now you're becoming more like him."

I couldn't believe that Mom wanted Michael to be more like me. I didn't know what to say, so I just took another huge bite of my sandwich. Thankfully, Mom dropped the subject.

After I'd finished my sandwich, I went over to the TV and grabbed my sneakers and put them back in the closet. Boy, mothers were hard to figure out. I thought she missed having sneakers thrown around the house.

I left the house and ran back to the pool. It was a relief to hide my hair under a bathing cap. Sometimes I worry that bits are going to escape from beneath the scarf.

Coach Jordan was there for the afternoon practice. She had the girls compete against the boys. I really liked challenging the boys because it made me try even harder. But I didn't like it when Joe Finnegan raced against me—and won. He laughed at me, and then he cupped his hand in the water and squirted me right in the face.

After practice, Coach Jordan pulled me aside.

"Cassie, I've noticed the great improvement you've made in your swimming. You've come a long way, and you should be proud of yourself," she said with a smile.

Then she handed me a white ribbon with a gold paper star stuck on at the top. "I've selected you as Swimmer of the Week for making the most personal progress."

"Yeah!" cheered Robin. She knew how important winning a ribbon was to me.

I looked around at the rest of the team who clapped and whistled. I could hardly believe this was happening to me. Sometimes it seems that a ton of good stuff happens at the same time. Boy, it was turning out to be a great day!

"Congratulations!" said Robin, patting me on the back as we walked into the locker room.

I was careful to keep the white ribbon away from my swimsuit so it wouldn't get wet.

"And I've got more good news—I can come over to your house after dinner," I said to Robin. Then, without another word, I threw on my clothes and hurried from Swimland. I jogged all the way home. I was excited to see Dad's car in the driveway when I got there.

Both Mom and Dad would be able to see my ribbon at the same time!

I burst in through the front door and galloped into the house. Mom was on the telephone in the kitchen. I heard Dad's voice coming from upstairs. He was talking on the extension phone in the bedroom.

I waited eagerly for Mom to hang up. I was so excited that I could hardly stand the wait. Finally, I calmed down enough to listen to what Mom was saying.

"Why, Michael! Congratulations! That's wonderful! You beat the camp record by how much? That's great that your name will go into their record books, too. Uh-huh. Uh-huh. Sure. We'll see you in just a few days. Good-bye."

Dad's heavy footsteps came down the stairs. His voice boomed, "That's our boy, Diane. He's breaking records all over the place," he said as he entered the kitchen. "Hi, Cassie. Did you hear the good news about

Michael?" Dad grinned from ear-to-ear.

Mom turned to wink at me. "He could be heading for the Olympics," she said with a big sigh. "Wouldn't that be great?"

I nodded my head silently and pushed the white ribbon down into the deepest corner of my shorts' pocket. After all, I hadn't won a race or broken a record. It was only a little ribbon with a paper star on it.

Four

I decided not to let Michael's phone call get me down. Sure, Michael broke records. But I was just learning to swim, and I'm much younger. There will be lots of chances for me to win ribbons and set records. I mean, look how fast I won my first ribbon!

If I just could get rid of my green hair, everything would be great.

Dad drove me over to Robin's house after dinner.

Robin was almost as excited as I was about dying my hair as we walked over to the drug store. We found the aisle that had all the shampoo, conditioners, and dyes. You wouldn't believe all the stuff you can buy to put on your hair. There are creams and sprays to make your hair soft, stiff, curly, or straight.

"Here it is!" exclaimed Robin. "Hey, this looks like your color, doesn't it? It's called Autumn Sun."

I inspected the box closely. On the front was a picture of a gorgeous model with her long hair brushed over half of her face. Her hair fell in dark blond waves with just a hint of golden highlight.

Her hair was beautiful. It reminded me of how my hair used to look. But I have to admit that the model's hair still was prettier than mine ever was.

"Autumn Sun," I said, reading the box. "It's a nice color."

On the back of the box it said "It's as easy as one-two-three! Just apply the tint, wait, and shampoo! Your hair will thank you for it!"

"This is it!" I announced. "It's perfect!"

I paid for the package at the front counter. "If it works, this will be the best five dollars that I've ever spent!" I exclaimed as Robin and I left the store.

I was so excited that I ran ahead, and Robin finally called, "Wait up, Cassie! Slow down!"

I kept thinking of the beautiful model on the front of the box. Robin and I finally reached her house. We walked inside and saw that her parents were busy watching a comedy show on TV. We quietly crept up the stairs to the bathroom and opened the box.

Robin grabbed a few towels from the cupboard and began reading the directions. I took the two bottles from the box and opened them. As Robin read the steps of what to do, I mixed together the dye and peroxide in an empty bottle. Little powdery swirls of orange color floated throughout the water.

"Hmm," I said. "That doesn't look very dark."

"But the directions say to use only a little bit of dye," Robin said as she read the directions again.

"But I need more than that if I'm going to

cover up the green," I explained.

Robin watched as I dropped more dye into the bottle.

"Now that's more like it!" I exclaimed. The water in the bottle was turning a dark, golden, orangy color. I leaned forward over the sink as Robin carefully worked the dye into my hair.

"Hey," I said. "That feels good."

"Hmm," said Robin. "Maybe I should become a hair stylist."

"Yeah," I agreed with a giggle. "You could specialize in people with green hair."

"Give me a break," said Robin. "Okay, stand up. Now put this thing on your head." She handed me a clear plastic shower cap. I stuffed my hair up under it.

Then I looked at Robin's hands. Orange dye dripped from her fingertips. "I sure hope I don't end up having red hair," I said.

"What's wrong with having red hair?" asked Robin, patting her own red curls. She looked a little hurt by my comment.

"Nothing's wrong with having red hair," I hurried to explain. "It's just that I want my own hair back."

Robin glanced at her watch. "It's supposed to stay on for 25 minutes," she said. "Then we shampoo it out."

In just 25 minutes, I'd look normal again, I thought. I couldn't wait!

Robin and I sat down on her bedroom floor to wait. I teased her about boys, and we looked through a new teen magazine that she'd just bought. So, I wasn't quite a teen yet. I was close enough!

After a few minutes, I pulled a strand of hair out from under my cap. Looking at it closely, I said, "I don't see any change yet."

"You have to wait 25 minutes," explained Robin.

When the time was up, I walked to the mirror and carefully took the cap off of my head. I was very disappointed. There was hardly any change at all. It didn't even seem worth the trouble of rinsing out the dye.

"Maybe this dye isn't made for people with green hair," suggested Robin. "Your hair might need more time for the dye to work."

Now I was beginning to worry. This wasn't how it was supposed to go. I thought for sure this was the answer. I was determined to leave the dye on for a while longer. It just had to work!

By the time we decided to go to bed, my hair was completely dry beneath the cap. I felt it with my fingers. But I decided to leave the dye on all night. I was sure that would do the trick.

"You might end up with super blond hair," Robin cautioned.

"That's fine by me. It's better than having green hair," I said grimly.

Just before I fell asleep, I thought of a fairy tale. My life seemed like the story of *The Ugly Duckling*, where the baby bird thinks he's really ugly. Then one morning he discovers he's a beautiful swan. It's just the same way with me. I was falling asleep with a head of green hair. But I was sure that the next morning I'd wake up with golden hair again.

I woke up the next morning because Robin was frantically shaking my shoulder.

"Let's see it!" Robin squealed.

"Huh?" I said as I sat up in bed, rubbing my eyes. Then I remembered my hair and jumped out of bed and ran to the bathroom with Robin. I pulled the cap off of my head and saw that my hair had dried in dark clumps and strands.

"It won't look right until we shampoo it out," assured Robin. But I could tell from her face that she was worried.

I bent over the sink and ran water over my head. Streams of colored water flowed from my head and down the drain.

"Look!" I exclaimed. "The water's turning green. The green's coming out of my hair!"

Robin didn't say a word. She stared solemnly at me as I vigorously rubbed my hair with a towel. Standing up, I looked in the mirror. I almost screamed at what I saw. The reflection staring back at me was a girl with bright green hair. Robin's face looked just like mine. But her hair didn't look like horror night in the snake pit like mine did!

"Oh, no!" I screamed. My heart began to pound. This couldn't be happening to me. My hair was the color of summer grass. I'd rather have my old pea soup hair back. Maybe that hadn't been such a bad color, after all.

"What am I going to do?" I wailed.

Robin put her hand up over her mouth. I could tell that she was trying not to laugh, which made me feel even worse. A few snorts and giggles leaked out from behind her hand.

"I'm sorry, Cassie," Robin struggled to say. "It's just that your hair is so...so....green!"

"What am I going to do?" I moaned. "I can't go home like this. Mom and Dad will have multiple heart attacks!"

Robin said, "You could join a sea aquarium and get a job as a performing mermaid. They have green hair, don't they?"

I scowled at Robin, and she grew quiet. After a few minutes, she asked, "Okay, how about if I cut your hair for you? Maybe it wouldn't look so green if it was shorter."

"Do you really think so?" I asked hopefully. I was willing to try almost anything.

"You said I'd make a good hair stylist, didn't you?" asked Robin. She ran from the room, then returned with a pair of sharp scissors. I sat down in front of her mirror. She draped a towel over my shoulders.

"Are you sure you know what you're doing?" I asked.

"Trust me," said Robin. "It can't look any worse than it already does, can it?"

I had to agree with her. As she snipped away with the scissors, I saw long, wavy strands of green hair fall to the floor. I've had long hair for as long as I can remember. It was weird to see the tips of my ears poking out from under the short pieces of hair.

"You're not taking too much off, are you?" I asked, worriedly. I was beginning to resemble a green porcupine.

Robin stood back, inspecting me in the mirror. "It'll look better when we curl it," she said.

"There's not much left to curl," I complained. I ran a hand over my head. Short spiky bits of hair poked this way and that.

Next, we tried the electric rollers. After Robin took them out, she brushed my hair and tried to flip it this way and that. Then, she stepped back and stared at me.

She said, "There! That's much better!"

"Are you kidding?" I shrieked.

Looking back at me was a curly, green-headed girl. And she didn't look better. She looked far from better.

"I look like a frog!" I yelled.

Five

WHAT was I going to do now? Mom and Dad were going to be mad for sure. I looked like an alien fresh off a U.F.O. I'm sure that's not the kind of daughter they would be proud of.

My stomach was in knots. I felt like I was going to be sick. I'd been so sure that our plan to dye my hair would work. I could just kick myself. But that wouldn't help anything now. What could I do? There was no way that I could go home.

I called home, and Mom answered on the second ring.

"Hi, Mom. Robin and I are having lots of fun. And I wondered if I could spend one more night here. She has some stuff she wants me to help her with," I said in one big breath.

"Certainly not!" exclaimed my mom. "Cassie, you've spent enough time there. I want you home in time for dinner tonight. We like to see you sometimes, too."

"Oh, gee, Mom," I said. "Do I have to?"

"I'll see you at dinnertime," Mom said. She was using her you-better-not-argue voice.

"Okay," I said, with a sigh. "I'll be home later," I finished and then hung up.

Suddenly, Robin's mom was calling us down to breakfast. "Robin! Cassie! Breakfast is ready."

Robin and I stared into each other's eyes in panic. Then quickly Robin reached into her gym bag and pulled out her bathing cap. "Here!" she said. "Put this on!"

I pulled the white elastic cap down snugly over my head. It was a lot easier to do without all the hair I used to have. I gazed regretfully into Robin's wastebasket where my freshly cut

50

green hair still sat.

Robin and I walked out into the hallway and toward the stairs. But I stopped abruptly in the hallway. "I can't go to breakfast with this thing on my head," I whispered. "Your mom will think I'm wacko or something."

"But she'll *know* you've gone wacko if she sees your hair," Robin whispered back.

I slowly followed Robin downstairs to the kitchen. The smell of eggs and bacon made my stomach grumble. Anxiously, I sat down at the table and waited for Mrs. Schuman to look at me. When she turned around from the stove, she did a double-take.

"Cassie?" she asked. "Isn't that a swimming cap on your head?" She looked puzzled.

I ran my hand over the top of my head, feeling the rubber cap. "Yes, Mrs. Schuman," I said. "It's a bathing cap, all right."

Just then Robin's dad walked into the kitchen. He glanced at me and smiled. "Why the swim cap, Cassie?" he asked. "Is it some kind of initiation? Have you joined a club?"

He shook his head, and his eyes twinkled. "That's the kind of crazy thing we always did when we were kids," he chuckled.

Suddenly, I realized that that was it! That could be my way out!

"Yes," I said slowly. "It's an initiation. It's for the Aqua Bears. We have to wear bathing caps on our heads at all times."

"That's strange," said Mrs. Schuman. "Then why aren't you wearing a bathing cap, Robin? You're still on the swim team, aren't you?"

Robin's eyes widened in shock. "I...I..."

"Robin has to wear a cap next week," I said quickly. "People get initiated into the Aqua Bears one at a time."

"Yum!" said Robin. "I love scrambled eggs." I could tell that she was trying to change the subject.

"Yeah," I chimed in. "The bacon smells great."

Soon we were all busy eating, and no one seemed to notice my white, rubbery head anymore. After breakfast, Robin and I quickly left the kitchen and went back up to her room.

I flopped down on Robin's bed. "So, what do I do now?" I asked.

Robin thought for a moment. "My grandmother gave me an old wig of hers to use for my Halloween costume. You can wear it if you want to," she said.

At that point, just about anything was worth a try. "Okay," I said. "Let me see what it looks like."

Robin raced from the room and returned with a large wig box. She lifted the top from the box and pulled out the wig.

"Eew! Gross! It's gray!" I exclaimed in horror.

"Well, my grandmother has gray hair," explained Robin. "But it might be better than nothing."

I sat in front of Robin's mirror and pulled

the bathing cap off my head. My hair looked worse than ever—green and mashed down, sort of like the canned spinach we get at school on bad days.

Quickly, I pulled the wig over my head. It fit loosely. As I walked over to look into Robin's big mirror, Robin started to giggle.

"This looks terrible," I moaned, staring at myself.

I took the wig off and put it back in the box. I pulled the bathing cap back on. I figured wearing the cap was better than looking like a weird old lady.

"I hope this bathing cap doesn't squeeze my brain too tightly. I have enough problems now without shrinking my brain, too," I said.

Robin and I sat in her room, trying to come up with the perfect plot. But nothing came. *What I need is a miracle,* I decided.

"We better get over to the pool," I said. "That's the only place I can wear this cap without looking like a super freak."

We grabbed our gym bags and headed for Swimland. As we walked into the parking lot, Karl Bosley rode by on his bicycle.

"Hi, Robin. Hi, Cassie," he said as he pedaled by. "See you in the pool."

As Karl disappeared around the corner, Robin grinned and said, "I think I'm going to die! He spoke to me! The captain of the boys' team actually spoke to me!" Her eyes sparkled. It was sickening.

"You know, Cassie," she said to me with a big grin. "Maybe joining the Aqua Bears wasn't such a bad idea, after all."

I didn't share her excitement. After all, it was after I joined the Aqua Bears that everything started going wrong in my life. It began with green hair and seemed to be ending with even greener hair.

"Hey, Rubberhead!" called Joe Finnegan from behind us. He walked up beside us and stared at my head. "Gee," he said. "From a distance you look bald. Couldn't you even wait until you got into the pool to put your cap on?"

"Get lost!" I growled.

Joe took a final look at me, and then he headed for the pool.

"I never knew that being 12 years old could be so hard. I always thought the really crummy stuff didn't happen to you until you were a grown-up," I said to Robin.

Robin shrugged her shoulders. We went to the locker room and changed into our swimsuits. As soon as I jumped into the pool, I felt better. I was in the middle of a crowd of other swimmers who were all wearing bathing caps. There was nothing that made me stand out. What a relief! *Now, if only I could stay in the pool until my hair grows out,* I thought.

Coach Jordan paired us off to race against each other. The winners then raced other winners until finally there were two grand champions. Lanna Baker was by far the best swimmer on the girls' team. And Karl Bosley was still the best on the boys' team.

Then we swam laps. Some people might think that swimming laps is boring. But it gave me time to think. It felt good just to swim and think. It was the one time when all my problems seemed to melt away.

When Coach Jordan signaled the end of practice, Robin quickly climbed out of the pool. "Are you coming, Cassie?" she asked.

"Nah," I replied. "I think I'll stay and swim some more."

Robin lowered her voice. "Be careful, Cassie," she warned. "Swimming makes your shoulders big. Boys don't like girls with big shoulders." Robin grinned and waved good-bye as she headed for the locker room.

Only a few other people stayed in the pool after practice. I swam back and forth, doing the breaststroke, the backstroke, and freestyle. With each pull of my arms, and with each kick of my legs, I mentally chanted, "Green hair, go away! Green hair, go away!"

I must have swum a mile or more. When I finally stopped, I looked around me and discovered that I was the last person left in the pool.

"Uh-oh," I said to myself. "I'd better get home in time for dinner."

I jumped out of the pool and ran to the locker room where I changed into my clothes. I dried off the top of my bathing cap with my towel. As I left the locker room I caught a glimpse of myself in the mirror. I had to admit that Joe Finnegan was right. From a distance, I did look like I was bald.

Hurrying to get outside, I walked through the gate and began running. I couldn't afford to be in trouble, so I ran the whole way home. I finally slowed down when I reached my driveway. There was a strange car sitting there. *Uh-oh. What am I going to do now?* I wondered.

As soon as I stepped into the house, Mom's voice greeted me. I couldn't escape, so I walked into the family room.

"Cassie," Mom said. "I'd like for you to meet Mr. and Mrs. Haddick. And this is their daughter, Julie. She's almost five years old. The Haddicks are our new neighbors on the other side of the block. They just bought the Sugarmans' house."

I looked from Mr. Haddick to Mrs. Haddick. They smiled and stared back at me.

"What's on her head, Mommy?" asked the little girl.

"I was just about to ask the same question," my dad said.

Mom and Dad looked at me like I had gone nuts. That's when I explained the whole story about how I had to wear the bathing cap for one whole week as part of the Aqua Bears' initiation.

"I don't remember Michael doing anything like that when he swam at Swimland," said Mom.

"Well, that was a long time ago. It's different now," I answered.

"Doesn't she have any hair, Mommy?" asked the little girl.

Mrs. Haddick nodded her head. "I'm sure she does, Julie," she said.

My mother smiled and shook her head. "Cassie actually has very beautiful hair. It's long and blond. You'll have to come back next week and see what Cassie really looks like."

Mom wouldn't have said that if she knew the terrible secret that lurked beneath my bathing cap.

I followed the others into the dining room and took my place at the table. I felt pretty dumb sitting there with my head stuffed into a bathing cap. I could tell that Mr. and Mrs. Haddick were trying not to stare at me. But Julie was too little to know that staring is impolite. She just stared away.

"Mommy," the little girl said. "She looks like a volleyball."

All the grown-ups laughed, and I tried to

force a smile. I decided that manners should be a required subject in kindergarten. I was relieved when the discussion switched over to Michael and his fabulous life. I should've known it would sooner or later, anyway.

"Our son will be home in three days," Mom said. "We've really missed him around here."

I caught my breath. I had been so worried about my green hair that I didn't realize Michael would be home so soon. I had to think of something fast. Michael would take one look at me and know that something was wrong. He'd never fall for the Aqua Bears initiation story.

The future looked pretty grim. Michael would soon be home with a suitcase full of more medals and trophies. He was the wonderful son every parent longs to have. And then there's me—the average, green-haired, alien daughter.

Six

DINNER with the Haddicks was humiliating, but I survived. I could barely eat anything after hearing that Michael was coming home. I quickly excused myself after dinner, saying that I wanted to take a bath after the long day in the pool.

No one seemed to care that I left, except Julie, who continued to stare at me as I got up from the table.

The next morning was bright and sunny. I went out onto the front porch to do some thinking. I needed to come up with a plan—and FAST! Every few minutes, I stuck a finger underneath my bathing cap to let in some fresh air. I definitely did not need moldy hair.

Mom came outside carrying a glass of lemonade. "Cassie, why don't you take off that cap? You must be burning up."

"It's not so bad, Mom," I said, trying to force a smile. "Anyway, I have to keep it on for a few more days. It's the Aqua Bears rule."

"But, honey, none of them are around now. How will they know if you take it off for a while?" She looked at me like she had just come up with the perfect solution.

"Uh, because they might send a spy around to be sure I'm wearing it," I said. "Only two of us wear them this week, so they might be checking up on me."

Mom gave me a strange look and went back into the house. I sat gazing out at all the freshly cut yards around the neighborhood. The lawns all looked like my hair.

I hadn't had the courage to take off my cap since yesterday. Maybe I should check in case a miracle happened or something.

I went upstairs to my bedroom. After closing the door tightly behind me, I ripped the bathing cap off of my head. I ran my fingers through my short, damp hair. What a relief it was to let my head cool off. Then I slowly got up my courage and walked over to the mirror.

My hair was as green as ever. It looked exactly like that stuff they use in football stadiums when they don't have real grass.

It was then that I realized that I might miss out on sixth grade. School was only two months away, and my hair looked like it was going to be with me forever. There was no way that I could go back to school with hair like this. Kids like Joe Finnegan would call me Turf Brain or worse.

Suddenly, there was a knock at my door. "Cassie?" Mom called through the door. "Robin is on the telephone."

I frantically grabbed my swim cap and pulled it down over my ears. Then I went to answer the phone in Mom and Dad's bedroom.

"Hello?" I answered.

"Let's go to the mall for ice cream," Robin suggested. "Mom said she'd drive us."

"Are you serious?" I asked. "I can't go to the mall with a swim cap on my head. Everyone will think I'm strange."

Robin paused a second, and then she said, "You know, Cassie. Maybe your hair doesn't look as bad as you think it does."

"What do you mean?" I could hardly believe what I was hearing.

"Why don't you come to the mall with your real hair?" Robin suggested seriously.

I thought she must be going crazy to suggest such a stupid idea.

"You can take the cap off when we get there so my mother won't know. It's crowded at the mall. And we probably won't see anyone we know. I'll bet no one will even notice your hair," Robin said.

"Do you really think so?" I asked hopefully.

"Honest," said Robin. "We'll be by to pick you up in 15 minutes, okay?"

"Okay!" I exclaimed and hung up the phone. I was filled with a mixture of excitement and fear. Maybe my hair didn't look so bad, after all. If Robin had said my hair wasn't so bad, then maybe it wasn't. My best friend wouldn't suggest something that would humiliate me, would she?

But what if people did laugh? What if everyone in the whole mall suddenly pointed at me and started laughing? It was a chance I had to take. I couldn't wait to be the real me again.

A few minutes later I heard Mrs. Schuman pull into the driveway. I made sure that my bathing cap was firmly in place, and then I ran out and climbed into the backseat of the car. Robin sat in the front seat beside her mom. She turned around and gave me a wink.

"Oh, are you still being initiated, dear?" Mrs. Schuman asked.

"Yes, ma'am," I replied.

"When did you say it's your turn, Robin?"

Mrs. Schuman asked.

"Uh, not until next week," Robin said quickly. Then she shot me a panicked look.

When we got to the mall, Mrs. Schuman told us when and where to meet her. Then she walked into a dress store.

Robin and I found a public restroom and quickly ducked inside to get rid of my bathing cap.

As soon as I pulled off my cap, I felt sick. How in the world was this going to work? My green hair was matted down with sweat. Bits and pieces of hair poked out in all directions. In fact, I felt a little bit like the Statue of Liberty, except my head was surrounded by spikes instead of a wreath.

Robin took a comb from her purse and ran it through my hair. "There," she said. "That's better."

I looked doubtfully at my reflection. I didn't see any difference. "Are you sure?" I asked.

"Sure, I'm sure," Robin said reassuringly.

"Maybe people will think it's a new style," I offered hopefully.

I gulped back my nervousness and left the bathroom with Robin. It felt good to have my cap off for a while. My head felt like it had just been let out of prison.

People seemed to be hurrying everywhere. Some carried packages. Others held the hands of small children. And other people seemed to be window shopping.

As Robin and I walked along, a few people stared at me. But most of them just smiled and looked away. It was a relief to discover that my hair didn't make anyone faint.

Robin and I kept an eye out for her mother as we made our way to the Ice Cream Shoppe. The girl behind the counter didn't blink an eye as I stepped up to place my order. It was wonderful to feel normal again. Only a few people stared at me, and they were mainly little kids or old people.

Coconut ice cream is my favorite, and my

double dip was gone in about three minutes.

"Ooo!" squealed Robin, as she crunched on the last bite of her cone. "Look at that dress in the window over there. I want to try it on!"

I followed Robin into a clothing store. She found the dress on a rack and disappeared with it into a fitting room. I looked at an earring display while I waited for her.

"Cool hair!" someone behind me said.

I whirled around to find a group of kids staring at me. They looked like they were a little older than I was. My eyes widened in shock as I checked them out. The girl who stood right in front of me had bright orange spiked hair. It looked like the tips of the spikes had been dipped in blue ink. And she had drawn big black circles around her eyes.

Another girl stepped forward. Her teeth looked yellow against the white lipstick she had on. "Wow! How'd you get your hair so green? It's so ugly that it's beautiful!"

All the other kids in the group stood there

nodding at me. Most of them were wearing black, silver-studded belts. They were definitely weird-looking.

A girl with purple hair pointed to my T-shirt and shorts. "Your clothes are boring," she said. "But your hair is totally cool!"

"It's looks like goose gizzards!" said the white-lipped girl.

A salesclerk walked by, frowning at all of us. I didn't know what to say. I was embarrassed to be considered part of this group. I wondered if I looked as strange as these girls did.

Robin waltzed out of the fitting room in a white and red summer dress. "How does it look?" she asked. She stopped short when she saw the group that I was standing with.

"It looks boring," said the purple-haired girl. "See if they have it in leather."

"She looks like my grandmother," whispered the girl with white lips. Then she turned to me and asked, "You're cool. But why is your friend so weird?"

I ran my hand across my green, spiky hair. "I—it was an accident," I stammered. "I never really wanted to have green hair."

"So, you're boring, too," said the purple-haired girl.

"Definitely," said the other girls. They turned and walked away, clanking and jingling with every step.

"What was that all about?" Robin asked.

A lump rose to my throat. "They thought I was one of them. They liked my hair," I told her.

I rushed into the nearest fitting room and pulled the bathing cap out of my purse. I yanked it onto my head and looked in the mirror. It looked strange, but it was better than what had just happened.

"Gee," said Robin, following me into the little room. "I guess my idea wasn't so great, after all. But, Cassie, you know that everyone will stare at you just as much with a bathing cap on your head."

"I'm never going anywhere in public again as long as I live," I said with determination. "My only hope is that my hair would all grow out blond someday. But the new hair will turn green too, unless I give up swimming. Oh, what am I going to do?"

Robin just stared at me helplessly. I glanced at myself once more in the mirror before I walked out into the store. As I stepped back out into the mall, people began to stare again. I hoped that they would think I'd had brain surgery.

It seemed like years before we finally met up again with Mrs. Schuman. I didn't say much as we drove out of the mall parking lot. My head was buzzing with problems—those weird kids, my brother, school, swimming, medals, Mom and Dad.

I thought about how grown-ups always say that they wish they could be kids again. All I can say is that they are crazy.

Seven

ALL afternoon I just sat around my room and tried to think up a solution to all my problems. I considered shaving my head and starting to grow my hair over. No, I had to think of another idea.

As a last resort, I even thought about telling Mom that she had a super-freak, green-haired daughter. But after trying so hard to make her proud of me—even just a little—I couldn't tell her what a stupid mess I'd gotten myself into. So, instead, I told Mom I wasn't feeling well and went to bed early.

The next morning I woke up before anyone else. I sat in my room wishing that a one-way space shuttle ticket would appear and announce that I was going to Jupiter. I figured that the aliens on Jupiter would accept my green hair. *What a great idea!* I thought.

I let my mind wander. Is there really a place in the world where green-haired people can live with brunettes and blonds—and not be made fun of all the time?

My ideas quickly faded away as I heard the doorbell ring. I wondered if it was Robin already. *But it's kind of early to go to Swimland now,* I thought.

A moment later, my mom called up to me, "Cassie, Robin's here!"

I poked my head out into the hall. "Come on up!" I yelled.

Robin came bounding up the stairs with a big sack under her arm.

"What do you have in there?" I asked curiously.

"It's the answer to all your problems," Robin said in a whisper.

I looked skeptically at the bag. After all,

Robin's good ideas had gotten me into even more trouble lately. There was her idea to use the hair dye that turned my hair even greener. Then there was the haircut that left me looking like a chicken fight had occurred on my head. And, of course, there was the great martian at the mall plan.

Robin reached into her bag and pulled out a hat. She held it up for me to inspect. I saw that it was woven from straw.

"It's pretty," I said, looking suspiciously at Robin. "What's the catch?"

"Put it on!" Robin exclaimed.

I snatched the bathing cap from my head and walked over to my mirror. I set the straw hat on my head and tied the sashes beneath my chin.

Robin stood silently behind me as I inspected myself from every angle. My green hair was completely hidden from sight. And my scalp felt a lot better now that the sweaty bathing cap was off.

"What do you think?" Robin asked, smiling.

"It's great!" I exclaimed. All of a sudden, I didn't feel like a freak anymore. With the hat on my head, I even looked fairly stylish.

"I got it this morning," Robin said. "Mom and I went shopping. As soon as I saw it, I thought of you. Isn't it cute?"

There was a knock at my door, and Mom poked her head inside. "Cassie, it's almost time for swim practice," she said. "Oh, what a nice hat. Where did you get it?"

"It's a birthday present from me," said Robin.

Mom's eyebrows dipped. "But Cassie's birthday is four months away," she said.

"It's an early birthday present," Robin replied. "I saw it at the mall and thought she'd like it."

Mom nodded her head as she inspected me. "It's nice to see you in something besides that bathing cap," she said. "But what about your

initiation? Can you substitute a hat for the bathing cap?"

"Uh, yeah. They said if the cap gets really gross, you can wear a hat for a while," I answered quickly.

Then Mom closed the door, and I heard her footsteps as she walked back downstairs.

I hugged Robin. "Thanks!" I exclaimed. "Now I can go outside without feeling like an idiot. You've saved my life!"

I grabbed my gym bag. Robin and I hurried downstairs and began the walk to Swimland. Or, rather, I began my traditional run to Swimland.

"Wait up, Cassie," called Robin. "Quit running. There's no way that I can keep up with you when you run everywhere."

I slowed down to wait for Robin. I always forget that she hates to run. It's amazing that I've gotten so used to running. I'm actually starting to enjoy the runs between home and the pool. But it seems like I run into Joe

Finnegan in the Swimland parking lot just about every day. And that day was no different.

"Hey, Melonhead!" he yelled at me. "What's with the new hat?"

Struggling to ignore him, I continued walking toward the main door. But Joe rushed up beside me.

"How come you wore a cap the other day and a hat today?" he asked suspiciously. "Are you trying to hide something?"

Joe reached for my hat. His fingers touched the brim. Robin shrieked as I pushed Joe's hand away. "Keep your paws off my hat," I growled. I tried to look calm.

Robin and I hurried to the locker room where we changed into our swimsuits. No one else was around, so I quickly put my new hat into my locker and pulled on my swim cap.

We joined the others in the pool, and Coach Jordan had us do some swimming exercises to strengthen our leg muscles. After about 30 minutes, she asked each of us to pick our best stroke. Two at a time, we swam two lengths of the pool. I guess she wanted to see how much we had improved.

I swam the breaststroke back and forth across the pool. I stopped for a moment to catch my breath. Joe Finnegan stopped beside me.

"What stroke are you swimming?" he asked with a grin. "It doesn't look like one I know."

I kicked him under the water. I admit it wasn't much of a kick because the water resistance held my leg back. But it was enough to make Joe yell.

I pushed off from the side of the pool and continued swimming my laps. When I reached the other end of the pool, Karl Bosley stopped beside me.

"Was Joe bothering you?" Karl asked me.

"It wasn't anything that I couldn't handle," I said.

Karl shot a glance across the pool at Joe.

He said, "Joe's an okay guy most of the time. He's just immature."

"That's for sure," I responded.

Karl laughed. Robin swam over to us, looking from my face to Karl's.

"What's so funny?" she asked.

I nodded my head toward Joe, who had just completed another lap. "He's what's so funny," I said.

Robin just stared at Karl and began to giggle. I pushed off from the side again and continued swimming.

When practice was over, Coach Jordan called us all together. "I've gone over all of your swimming times, and I have decided who will swim in the meet that is coming up," she said.

My heart jumped at the news. I could feel it beating fast as I waited for Coach Jordan to continue.

"Those of you who don't have qualifying times should not be disappointed at all. Every one of you has made great progress in your style and skill level. Keep at it, and you'll have a good shot at another meet," she said enthusiastically.

I gulped back a wave of nerves. Coach Jordan held a list in her hand. She read off the names of the boys who would be competing first. Karl Bosley, of course, was picked to swim in several events.

When Coach Jordan began reading down the girls' list, I crossed my fingers. Hopes of medals and trophies danced in my head. *If I get to swim in this meet, Mom and Dad will be so proud of me*, I thought. Coach Jordan rattled off the names. Finally, she came to the breaststroke.

"In the breaststroke," announced Coach Jordan, "it will be Lanna Baker."

Disappointment whirled through me. I felt my face muscles fall like they do whenever something rotten happens.

I hardly listened as Coach Jordan read the rest of the names. Then I shook Lanna Baker's hand because I didn't want to be thought of as a sore loser. But I admit that I felt like one. I really felt crummy.

Robin didn't care at all about not being chosen. As we walked back to the locker room, she whispered, "I'm glad I wasn't chosen. I don't think I could swim against some total stranger in another pool. I'd be too nervous."

The sight of the straw hat in my locker cheered me up a little. After all, with that hat, I almost looked like a normal human being. I replaced my swim cap with the straw hat and tied it firmly under my chin. In fact, I tied it in a double knot, because you never know when someone like Joe Finnegan is going to pull your hat off for all the world to see.

I ran all the way home. When I got there, Mom was on the phone with Michael—of course.

"We miss you, too, dear," she was saying. "Yes, we'll see you tomorrow. Oh, Cassie just walked in!"

Mom pushed the receiver at me, and I reluctantly took it. "Hi Michael," I said. "How's camp?"

"It's pretty good," he replied. I admit it was good to hear his voice. "I've learned a lot. Hey, I hear you joined the Aqua Bears. That's great! I'm really proud of you, Cass."

I sighed deeply, thinking that Michael wouldn't be so proud if he knew that my times hadn't been good enough to even swim in a meet. "It'll be nice to be home again," said Michael. "Sleeping in bunk beds gets old after a while. Take it easy, Cass. I'll see you soon. Bye."

"Bye," I said and hung up the phone.

"He sounds good, doesn't he?" asked Mom.

"Yeah," I agreed. Then I went upstairs and hung my swimsuit in the bathroom to dry. I sat down in front of my bedroom mirror. It seemed like I was spending a lot of time there lately. I removed the straw hat and looked closely at my reflection. It wasn't a pretty sight.

My hair was as green as ever, kind of like the color of lime punch but darker. My eyes were bloodshot from the chlorine, and they were covered with tiny lines that looked like red road maps. Red marks from my goggles circled around my eyes. I looked like a kind of Christmas monster—colorful, but ugly.

What will Michael think when he sees me? He'll be embarrassed to have a sister with green hair. And then he won't want me to visit him at college next year. Michael won't want his college friends to know his sister is a freak. What'll I do? Somebody please help me!

The reflection in the mirror grew misty. I couldn't hold back the sobs any longer.

Eight

A T dinner that night, Mom and Dad did most of the talking. Mom passed along to Dad all the news about Michael. And Dad told us about his day.

They finally noticed that I wasn't saying much.

"You're awfully quiet tonight, Cassie," Dad said as he passed me the milk.

I just shrugged my shoulders like it was no big deal. I couldn't think of anything to say. After all, I couldn't tell them I wasn't chosen to swim in the next meet. And I couldn't tell them about my awful hair. So, what else was there to say? How could I confess all my failures when my brother was such a success?

"How is everything going with the Aqua Bears?" asked Mom.

"Okay," I mumbled and took a mouthful of food.

"That's a nice hat you've got there, Cassie," said Dad with a smile.

I forced a smile. "Thanks," I said.

"Are you all right, honey?" asked Mom. "You look tired."

"I am tired," I admitted with a nod. One thing I've learned from all of this is that green-haired people don't sleep well. Mostly they lie awake and worry. At least, that's what I do.

I excused myself from the table and carried my dishes to the kitchen. As I walked over to the sink, I noticed a box sitting on the counter. It was blue and red with bold black lettering on the front that said "WHAM-O laundry detergent gets rid of even the toughest stains."

I grabbed the box and read the back cover. It said "Will remove the following stains: blood, dirt, oil, grease, chocolate, and many more!"

This could be the answer! I thought. I wondered if green hair dye fell into the category of "many more." I mean, green hair is a stain—a BIG stain—isn't it? Anything was possible. And, besides, what could I possibly lose? Well, maybe all of my hair, but I wondered if that would be so bad at this point.

I shook some of the white soap powder into a plastic sandwich bag. Then I stuffed it into my pocket and went upstairs to the bathroom. I filled the sink almost full with warm water and then slowly dunked my head into the gross mixture.

Carefully, I sprinkled some WHAM-O onto my hair. It smelled good, kind of like clean sheets. I scrubbed and scrubbed. I kept looking at the water to see if anything was happening. More than anything, I wanted to see the green magically flowing off of my skull.

I shook the rest of the WHAM-O onto my scalp and rubbed it in as hard as I could. I

even took a toe nail brush from the tub and used it to scrub my head. I know that's gross, but wouldn't you try it if you had green hair?

At last, I rinsed the soap out and checked my hair in the mirror. The girl staring back at me still had green hair.

Then the answer came to me. I could join the circus and go on tour. Lots of people would pay to see a green-haired girl. But then I figured that my parents wouldn't allow me to travel without them.

Looking closely at my head, I saw that my scalp was red from all of the rubbing and soap suds. It felt sore. My red skin looked awful next to my green hair. It looked like monster makeup for Halloween or a late night horror movie.

There was a knock at the bathroom door. "Are you almost done in there?" Mom asked.

I quickly put the hat back onto my head. "I'll be right out," I called to her.

I rinsed out the sink and put the towels

back on the rack. Then I tied the strap beneath my chin, so the hat wouldn't slide off
my wet head. When I opened the bathroom
door, Mom stood there staring at me. *Uh-oh.
Had she discovered my secret? Was my hair
sticking out from under the hat?* I wondered.

"Can I spend the night with Robin?" I
suddenly blurted out. It seemed to be the only
way to escape from my mom's strange looks.

Mom thought for a moment, and then she
shook her head. "You've been spending too
much time at the Schumans' lately," she said.
"We hardly see you anymore. I think you'd
better stay home tonight. Besides, you'll want
to be here tomorrow."

"What's going on tomorrow?" I asked.

"Michael's coming home tomorrow!" Mom
announced. "Don't you remember?"

"Oh, yeah, Michael," I said sadly.

I went into my room and got ready for bed.
I had to put the dumb old bathing cap back
on my head so I wouldn't crush the hat. I

decided that I couldn't stand much more of this.

I sat on my bed for a while, but I wasn't tired enough to go to sleep. Finally, I went to Mom and Dad's bedroom to use their phone. I dialed and was glad when Robin answered the phone.

"Hi, Cassie," she said. "What's new?"

"Nothing," I said. "I'm tired of all this hiding. I spend half my life at your house, at the pool, or in my bedroom, just so Mom and Dad won't find out what I did to my hair. And my head hurts from sleeping in this bathing cap."

"You know what you need?" asked Robin.

"What?" I asked, hesitantly, hoping that this wouldn't be another of Robin's wild schemes.

"You need to do something different," suggested Robin cheerfully. "You need something to get your mind off your hair. Ha-Ha. Get it—your *mind* off your *hair*?"

"Yeah, I get it. That's very funny, Robin. Now what could get my mind off this mess?" I asked suspiciously. "You're not talking about going to the mall again, are you?"

"No," Robin hurried to say. "I thought we could go to a movie tomorrow. There's a good one playing at Pixley's. It's *The Adventures of John Flynn and Little Nick.* It's about these two guys who get shipwrecked on a deserted island. They have to live in the trees and make friends with the monkeys."

"It sounds great," I said. "I wish I could go."

I heard Robin sigh. "You can go," she insisted. "You can wear the hat."

"In the movie theater?" I asked. "No one would be able to see over my head." Sometimes Robin was crazy.

"Why not?" Robin asked again. "Some of the guys wear hats, you know like ball caps and stuff. And there are always lots of guys there," she giggled.

I struggled to come up with a decision. I

wanted so badly to be normal again and to do normal things. But could I really risk going to something as public as a movie? After all, green-haired people are at great risk whenever they expose themselves to people. But it didn't seem fair for me to have to miss a good movie.

And what would I do if my hat fell off? What if the manager made me take my hat off? Everyone would laugh at me. I'd be the laughing stock of Crandall, California. I'd never be able to go anywhere in public again. My parents would find out, and they'd be disappointed in me—again.

"Do you want to hide in your room for the rest of your life?" asked Robin impatiently. "Trust me. No one will notice a thing. What could go wrong?"

That was easy for her to say.

"Okay," I said. "I'll go."

Nine

A S soon as I hung up the phone, I wondered why I had agreed to go with Robin.
I mean, why was I willing to risk so much to see a movie?

Dad had agreed to drive us to the movies. As we pulled out of the driveway, Dad stared at me for a minute before he spoke.

"Are you sure you don't want to stay home, Cassie? Michael should be arriving pretty soon, you know," he reminded me.

I gave it a full second's thought. No way did I want to be home so that Michael could laugh at me or tell me how dumb I am. He's the perfect one to do that, after all.

"No thanks, Dad," I said. "I'll see him later

when I come home. And Mrs. Schuman is picking us up after the movie."

Robin was waiting in her front yard when we arrived. She ran to the car and climbed into the backseat.

Five minutes later, Dad had dropped us off at Pixley's Theater. There was already a line of kids waiting to buy tickets. I patted my hat to make sure it was firmly in place. Then I waved good-bye to Dad and walked to the end of the line beside Robin.

Suddenly, I heard a familiar voice behind me. "Hey, Cassie, what are you hiding under the hat?" the voice called.

"Oh, no!" whispered Robin. "Joe Finnegan's here!"

Joe stood close to the front of the line. He pointed a finger, and everyone turned to stare at me. "That girl is bald!" he shouted.

Everyone in the line started laughing. I felt my face turn pink as I looked at Robin.

"Maybe this wasn't such a good idea,"

Robin admitted in a whisper. Why did she always decide these things when it was too late?

"She's bald!" Joe Finnegan yelled again.

Someone tapped me on the shoulder, and I turned to see Krissy Johnson, a girl in my class at school.

"Don't pay any attention to Joe," she said sweetly. "I've seen your hair before. And I think it's beautiful! Why don't you take your hat off and show everyone?"

I gulped. "Uh, no," I stammered. "I'm not going to take my hat off just to please Joe Finnegan," I said stubbornly.

Krissy nodded her head. "I don't blame you," she said.

When the ticket window opened, the line moved forward quickly. Everyone finally quit staring at me, and I breathed a sigh of relief.

Robin and I waited by the counter to buy some popcorn. I saw some boys I knew from school. They stood together in a cluster, looking at me, whispering, and laughing. That's not the sort of thing that makes you feel popular.

I wondered if I should go hide in the bathroom and sneak into the theater when the lights went off. But before I had time to dash into the bathroom, Robin grabbed my arm and pulled me inside.

We found some empty seats near the back. In no time at all, most of the seats had filled up.

"This must be a good movie," I whispered. "It seems like everyone is here."

"I know," said Robin cheerfully. She turned her head to each side to scan the crowd. "Look at all the boys!" she whispered. "Isn't this great?"

I didn't think it was so great. After all, if anyone's going to give you a hard time about having green hair, a boy will. I checked the knotted sash on my hat to make sure it was securely fastened under my chin.

At last, the lights dimmed, and the movie began. I breathed a sigh of relief. It was so dark in there that I could barely see the people around me.

It felt so good to be doing something fun. I relaxed finally and untied the sash on my hat. I mean, no one can tell what color my hair is in the dark, right? And everyone was too busy watching the movie to pay any attention to me.

I lifted the hat from my head. I glanced around to see if anyone was paying attention to me. They weren't. It was an exciting part in the movie, and no one seemed to care about my hat and my green hair.

I ran my fingers through the short, ragged clumps that were now my hair. It felt wonderful to be in public without a swim cap or a hat.

I leaned back in my seat and watched the movie. It was pretty funny. There were these two men who lived on a deserted island where no other human beings lived. It occurred to me that an island like that would be the perfect place for a green-haired person to live. After all, monkeys and parrots don't care what your hair looks like.

I munched on my popcorn and candy. It was two hours of fun, and I hadn't had much of that lately.

But toward the end of the movie, my worries came back. I started thinking about Michael. I wondered if he was home yet and if he would think I was being weird and guess something was up. Even worse, I bet his suitcase would be filled with wonderful medals and trophies. And I figured he'd want to know how many medals I'd won with the Aqua Bears. And then Mom and Dad would be disappointed in me again.

The two hours we spent watching the movie flew by. It seemed like no time at all before the movie ended and the credits flashed onto the screen. I grabbed the hat from my lap and set it on my head. As I pulled the sash ends down to tie them, I felt a hand fall heavily onto the top of my hat. I turned around and came face to face with Joe Finnegan.

The overhead lights blazed on as kids flowed into the aisles to leave the theater. A group of kids stopped to listen as I yelled at Joe.

"Get your hands off of my hat!" I shouted.

"I want to see what you're hiding!" said Joe with a hearty laugh. "Come on! We Aqua Bears should stick together. We shouldn't have secrets from each other!"

My fingers clenched the brim of my hat, struggling to keep it on my head. Robin jumped forward and pushed Joe. "Stop it!" she yelled.

But Joe hung onto my hat, and bit by bit I felt the hat pulling away from my head. With a mighty yank, Joe grabbed the hat, and it went sailing into the aisle.

For a second, Joe stood silently staring at

me. His eyes bugged out as if he'd seen a ghost. "Your hair is green," he replied in amazement.

Krissy Johnson stopped in the aisle. "Cassie!" she exclaimed. "What happened to your hair?"

Another boy spoke up. "It looks like the seaweed in my fish tank," he said. Then there was loud laughter from the crowd that had gathered around me.

Joe stood staring at me. "I'm sorry, Cassie," he said in a quiet voice. "I didn't know. I was just kidding. Do you have some kind of disease or something?"

I stood there for a moment, frozen and unable to move. Kids were pointing and laughing at me. Finally, I couldn't take it anymore. With all my strength, I raced up the aisle, through the lobby, and outside into the sunshine. I just wanted to go home.

Ten

MY life was not going well. I mean, can you think of anything worse than having green hair and running through your hometown for everyone to see? I can't.

I couldn't control my tears. They started streaming down my cheeks as I raced through the streets of Crandall. People walking on the sidewalks jumped out of my way as I came barreling past. They probably thought I was a maniac.

A group of little children pointed at me and began to scream as I approached them. They scattered into nearby yards, hiding behind bushes. Still sobbing, I ran as fast as I could. When you have green hair and people are

screaming and laughing at you, you don't slow down for anything!

The movie theater is about three miles away from my house. It was hard to breathe after running for a while, and my lungs felt like they were going to burst. But I forced myself to keep running. All the troubles of the last few days flashed through my mind.

There was the day I first noticed a greenish tint taking over my hair. Then I got my ingenious idea of wearing my bathing cap everywhere. And, of course, there was Robin's great idea to dye my hair back to its real color. Waking up to green pepper-colored hair was worse than anything else that has ever happened to me. It was even worse than seeing all of Michael's medals and trophies everywhere.

More tears flowed as I recalled Robin's grandmother's gray wig. Then there was the terrible haircut that only made things worse and that horrible trip to the shopping mall. And then there was the WHAM-O laundry detergent that didn't live up to its promise at all!

And now life was even worse. Everyone knew my secret. Almost every kid in Crandall had seen my green hair! I figured that I'd just have to move away. There was no choice. I'd have to shave my head and go to a new town where no one knew me.

Huffing and puffing, I turned down another street. My thighs ached, and it seemed as if I'd been running forever. But it's impossible to run away from your hair. As I reached my street, I felt sick.

I wondered what Mom and Dad would think when they saw my martian head.

They're so proud of Michael. But I never do anything to make them proud of me. I'm just average Cassie, who never does anything special—except turn her hair green for the world to see.

I'll bet Mom and Dad wish I was more like Michael. I'll bet they can't figure out why he's a good swimmer and I haven't even been in a meet.

I tried to think of somewhere I could escape to and hide out forever. But the last few days had taught me that there isn't any safe place for a green-haired girl.

At last, my house came into view. Out of the corner of my eye I saw our new neighbors, Mr. and Mrs. Haddick, in their front yard. They stared at me as I ran by huffing, puffing, and crying. I must have been an awful sight— ragged green hair, a runny nose, and red eyes.

I knew that by going into the house, my parents would know once and for all that their daughter is an alien. I choked back a sob as I realized that they could never really love me. How could they? Michael was the perfect one.

Turning up my driveway, I ran to the front door of my house. The door was locked. But I saw my reflection glaring back at me in the window.

Well, this is it, I thought as I walked around

the side of the house. I stopped walking when I saw Michael sprawled in one of the lawn chairs. He was busy chatting away with Mom and Dad, who seemed to be excited by everything he was saying. It figured.

All six eyes turned to stare at me. Dad reacted first by jumping out of his chair and nearly knocking it over. "Cassie!" he exclaimed. "What happened to your hair?"

Mom's face looked sick. "Cassie!" she cried. "What in the world did you do?"

Michael just sat there and stared. He didn't say a word.

Eleven

I T finally happened. They had seen me. I flopped down into a lawn chair as Mom, Dad, and Michael gathered around me.

At last, the whole humiliating story came out. As I explained how my hair had arrived at such an ugly state, the tears kept flowing. I may have broken the record for crying. It seemed like I had been crying for hours.

I told Mom and Dad about how I'd thought they would laugh at me and my hair. I felt especially bad when I confessed that the story about the Aqua Bears initiation wasn't true. I had never lied to my parents before that. But with green hair, I'd learned how to sneak around and make up stories. It's not something that I'm proud of.

Mom, Dad, and Michael listened quietly as I told the whole weird story. The corners of Michael's mouth twitched upward into a grin that made me feel even worse. I thought he was making fun of me like everyone else had.

"And I'll never be a good swimmer like Michael is," I sobbed. "I'm one of the worst swimmers on the Aqua Bears! I don't even like to swim. I should have quit a long time ago, but I wanted you to be proud of me, just like you're proud of Michael."

I looked from Dad to Mom and back. Mom looked sad, and that made me feel even worse. I was surprised when she knelt beside me and wrapped her arms around me. Dad squeezed my shoulder with his hand.

"I'm sorry," Mom said.

"You're sorry?" I asked in shock. "About what? I'm the one who makes all the dumb mistakes. I'm the one who can't swim."

Mom hugged me closer. She said quietly,

"If you don't feel loved, then I'm doing something wrong."

"We both are," Dad added. His voice was deep and serious. "Cassie," he said. "Your mother and I love you very much. We love you no matter what you do or don't do. And we are always proud of you."

"But I never do anything!" I exclaimed. "I never win ribbons or medals or trophies. And no one pays me to go to school. I'm just not smart like Michael is."

Mom ran her fingers gently through my short, prickly green hair. She smiled a little. "Cassie," she said. "Your father and I never expected you to be like Michael. Michael is Michael. And you are you. You and Michael are two different people. You shouldn't try to be like someone else. Your father and I love you just the way you are."

"You do?" I asked. I couldn't believe what I was hearing. I never expected them to understand in a million years. But they did.

"Of course, we love you," Mom said. "You don't have to do anything to earn our love."

"I don't?" I asked.

"Of course not," Mom said. "We give you our love because you are our child. You don't have to do anything to earn it."

It was hard to believe. "You mean you won't love me more if I'm super smart and win lots of awards like Michael?" I asked.

Mom shook her head. "We'll always be proud of you for your accomplishments," she said. "But our love stays the same—awards or no awards."

I wiped the tears from my face and took a deep breath. Then I gasped for air because that's what I do after I've cried really hard.

Michael had been standing there quietly. Finally, he leaned toward me and searched my face. "Gee, Cass," he said. "It sounds like you've been having a hard time. You know, you're pretty terrific all by yourself. Nobody needs two of me around. And, believe me, I'm far from perfect. That's for sure. Besides, I'd miss the old Cassie."

"You would?" I asked.

Nothing was turning out the way I'd thought it would. No one had screamed or fainted when they saw my hair. No one was disappointed or angry with me. In fact, they all cared. This was too good to be true.

My eyes welled with tears as I ran a hand over my head. "But what am I going to do about my hair?" I wailed. "School starts in two months, and I look like a frog!"

Mom smiled. "How about if we go together to the hair salon tomorrow?" she suggested. "Martha Jean can dye your hair back to its natural color. And she can cut your hair so it looks better."

I would never toss off compliments about my blond hair ever again. I couldn't wait to be blond again and to go out in public without panicking. There'd be no more swim caps, wigs, hats, or hiding.

I looked shyly at my brother. "I'm sorry, Michael," I said in a whisper.

He looked surprised. "Why are you sorry, Cass?" he asked.

I took a deep breath and confessed. "I'm sorry that I was so jealous of you. I wanted to have everything you have—brains and awards and everything. That was wrong. I should have been happier for you."

"That's okay, Cass," Michael said. He grinned at me. "You know," he said. "I haven't always been such a great guy. I made my share of mistakes when I was your age, and I still make mistakes."

Michael looked at Mom and Dad with a twinkle in his eye. "Remember the day I locked myself out of the house, and I had to go to the neighbors' house in my pajamas?" he asked.

Mom and Dad laughed at the memory.

"Remember the first time we took you out to dinner with us?" asked Mom. "You got so excited that you ate too much and too fast."

"And then you threw up all over the parking lot," added Dad.

"Michael barfed in a parking lot?" I asked. I couldn't hold back a grin. And just minutes before, I'd thought I could never smile again.

Michael looked embarrassed at the memory. "I sure did," he said. "There are all kinds of goofy things I did that you don't know about."

"Realizing that you make mistakes is part of being a grown-up," Mom said to me with a smile. "Everyone makes mistakes sometimes."

I leaned back in my chair, feeling much more relaxed. *I guess my family is all right, after all*, I thought.

"I think I'm going to quit the Aqua Bears," I said. "I'm just not meant to be a great swimmer."

"Maybe swimming isn't your sport, Cass," Michael said.

"Yeah, that's for sure," I answered with a sigh. "Hey, I did win a ribbon for Swimmer of the Week as most improved."

"When?" asked Mom. "You never showed it to us."

I didn't know what to say. "Well, you were talking to Michael on the phone when I got home, and then I forgot."

"That's great, Cassie," Michael said. "But besides winning ribbons, you have to enjoy swimming, too."

Just then, the phone rang. Dad got up to go answer it. A few minutes later, he came back outside and said it was Mr. Schuman asking if I was okay.

"Robin must have told him what happened. He probably thought I flipped out," I said. "I flew out of the theater like a complete idiot."

"So, how did you get home?" asked Michael.

"I ran," I said.

"You ran all the way home from Pixley's?" Michael asked. "That's at least three miles away from here."

"Yeah," I admitted. "And I thought I was

never going to make it home."

Michael smiled at me. "That's a long way to run at your age," he said. "Did you ever think of becoming a runner? There are lots of races of different distances. And running can be fun without competitions, too."

I gave that some thought. I *had* been running a lot lately. Maybe I *could* be a runner.

"I do love to run!" I exclaimed. "I ran to the pool every day this summer. And Robin's always telling me to slow down when I start running. Today I ran faster than I've ever run before. When you have green hair and you're running through Crandall, you don't slow down," I added with a grin.

Mom, Dad, and Michael laughed.

Mom took my hand. "Cassie, don't get carried away with running just because you think we don't love you. That shouldn't be part of your decision. Okay?"

I nodded my head. "Okay, Mom," I said. "But I really do like to run. I think it's something

I could be pretty good at. And even if I'm not the best, I guess that'd be okay, too."

Mom and Dad went into the house to make lemonade. But I know it was really just an excuse to leave Michael and me alone for a few minutes.

A light breeze ruffled my hair, and it felt good to let my head breathe again. I couldn't wait to be rid of this ragged, green mop. *Tomorrow, the whole green mess will be history*, I thought.

Michael leaned closer and patted my shoulder. "You're really something else," he said affectionately. "I think you're a great little sister. You know that now, don't you?"

I nodded. It took me a while, but I finally figured it out. I guess it was my green hair that taught me it's okay to be myself. Now I know that I don't have to prove anything to anyone. It's okay to be just a regular, average kid. That can be pretty special, too. And it's good enough for me!

About the Author

"I remember what it was like to be a kid," says JANET ADELE BLOSS. "I understand how kids feel things very deeply. And I know that kids love to laugh."

Anyone who reads Janet's books will agree that she has a keen insight into the emotional lives of children. The characters in her books live in a world of pesty sisters, creepy brothers, runaway pets, school bullies, and good friends.

The characters laugh, cry, dream, and race through the pages of her stories. As one reader says: "When I read your books, it's like I'm watching a movie."

Janet showed signs of becoming an author as early as third grade when she wrote a story entitled *Monkeys on the Moon.* By the time Janet reached fifth grade she had decided to become an author. She also wanted to be a flamenco dancer, a spy, a skater for roller derby, and a beach bum in California. But fortunately for her readers it was the dream of becoming an author that came true.

"I've always loved books and children," says Janet. "So writing for children is the perfect job for me. It's fun."

Although Janet's first love is writing, her other interests include dancing, music, camping, swimming, ice-skating, and cats.